Dinosaur Days

HarperCollins®, ■®, and HarperFestival® are trademarks of HarperCollins Publishers, Inc.

Harold and the Purple Crayon: Dinosaur Days

Text copyright © 2003 by Adelaide Productions, Inc. Illustrations copyright © 2003 by Adelaide Productions, Inc.

Printed in the U.S.A. All rights reserved. www.harperchildrens.com

Library of Congress Cataloging-in-Publication Data. Baker, Liza. Dinosaur Days/text by Liza Baker; illustrations by Andy Chiang.
p.   cm.—(Harold and the purple crayon) Based on a teleplay by Don Gillies.
Summary: When Harold is unable to sleep, he uses his purple crayon to draw a jungle in which he hopes to find dinosaurs.
ISBN 0-06-000541-6
[1. Drawing—Fiction.   2. Dinosaurs—Fiction.   3. Jungles—Fiction.   I. Chiang, Andy, ill.   II. Gillies, Don.   III. Title.   IV. Series.
PZ7.B17445 Di   2003   2002023309   [E]—dc21

Book design by Patrick Collins
1 2 3 4 5 6 7 8 9 10
❖
First Edition

HAROLD and the PURPLE CRAYON™

Dinosaur Days

Text by Liza Baker • Based on a teleplay by Don Gillies
Illustrations by Andy Chiang • Color by Sharon Matsumoto

HarperFestival®
A Division of HarperCollinsPublishers

One night Harold couldn't fall asleep.

In the dark he pulled out his flashlight and found his favorite book. It was all about dinosaurs— flying dinosaurs, spiky dinosaurs, and Harold's favorite kind of dinosaur: the big, long-necked kind.

I wonder what it would be like to ride on the back of a big, long-necked dinosaur, thought Harold. He decided to find out, with the help of his purple crayon.

Harold knew that some dinosaurs lived in the jungle.

Harold walked and walked under tall trees and
giant ferns. This jungle was full of strange surprises,
but he didn't see any big, long-necked dinosaurs.

Harold came to a roaring waterfall. He knew exactly how to get across it.

Harold drew a bridge.

Harold walked for a long time. He had seen many things in the jungle, but no dinosaurs.

The sun was shining and the jungle was hot. Harold's walk had tired him out. He sat down by a big rock.

But it wasn't a rock at all! It was a triceratops. Harold tried to make friends, but this triceratops wasn't very nice.

He decided that it was time to leave. Harold drew
a giant pterodactyl, and they flew off together.

The pterodactyl dropped him gently into her nest of eggs.

There was a *crack*, and one of the eggs hatched.
A baby pterodactyl climbed out.

Harold still wanted to meet a big, long-necked dinosaur, so he left the nest. The baby pterodactyl followed him down the mountain. Harold and the pterodactyl started to slip.

Harold quickly pulled out his crayon and drew
a vine. Together, they swung to safety.

Harold felt a strange rumbling under his feet.
He looked in the distance and saw...

...a volcano!

The volcano was erupting, so Harold and the baby pterodactyl ran as fast as they could.

Soon there were dinosaurs everywhere. The hot lava was catching up to them.

Harold acted quickly and drew a drain in the ground.
All the hot, oozing lava ran down the drain. Harold
and the dinosaurs thought they were safe.

Then there was a *crash*! A titanosaurus stomped out of the jungle. This was just the kind of big, long-necked dinosaur Harold had been searching for. But this dinosaur didn't look friendly.

The titanosaurus clomped closer and closer. He did not see the pool of black, sticky tar. He got stuck! Harold wanted to help him. He had an idea.

The titanosaurus was so happy to be free that he gave Harold and the baby pterodactyl a ride on his back. Harold finally got his wish.

After their ride, the mother pterodactyl came looking for her baby. It was time for him to go home.

I met a lot of dinosaurs, thought Harold. *Maybe it's time for me to go home, too.* He drew his bedroom window around the moon, and returned to his home.

Tucked safely in bed, Harold thought about all
of the dinosaurs he had met. Soon Harold's purple
crayon dropped to the floor, and Harold fell asleep.